Dedications

This book is about girls...finding the
greatness within...

It is dedicated to my daughters Elizabeth &
Caroline...and to my wife Leslie...who taught
them "greatness" — by example — since the
day they were born.
—Rick

To all the "girls" in my family who are
proving that GIRLS CAN!
—Marilyn

Library of Congress Cataloging-in-Publication Data

Kupchella, Rick, 1964-
    Girls Can / written by Rick Kupchella ; illustrated by Marilyn Brown.
       p. cm.
    Summary: Encourages girls to set their own course, knowing that they can do and be anything at all when they set their minds to it and
make it so. Briefly describes how Jackie Joyner-Kersee, Sandra Day O'Connor and Sally Ride achieved their dreams.
    ISBN 0-9726504-3-1 (alk. paper)
    [1. Sex role - Fiction. 2. Occupations - Fiction. 3. Self-realization - Fiction. 4. Individuality - Fiction. 5. Stories in rhyme.]
    I. Brown Marilyn, ill. II. Title

PZ8.3.K956 Gi 2004
[E] - dc22
2004048026

TRISTAN Publishing, Inc.
2300 Louisiana Avenue North, Suite B
Golden Valley, MN 55427

Text copyright © 2004 Rick Kupchella
Sandra Day O'Connor Photograph by Dave Penland,
Smithsonian Institution, Collection of the Supreme Court of the United States.
Jackie Joyner-Kersee Photograph by Tony Duffy

visit www.tristanpublishing.com

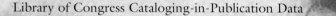

Girls Can!

Make it happen.

by Rick Kupchella
illustrated by Marilyn Brown

TRISTAN Publishing

Have I told you the story...

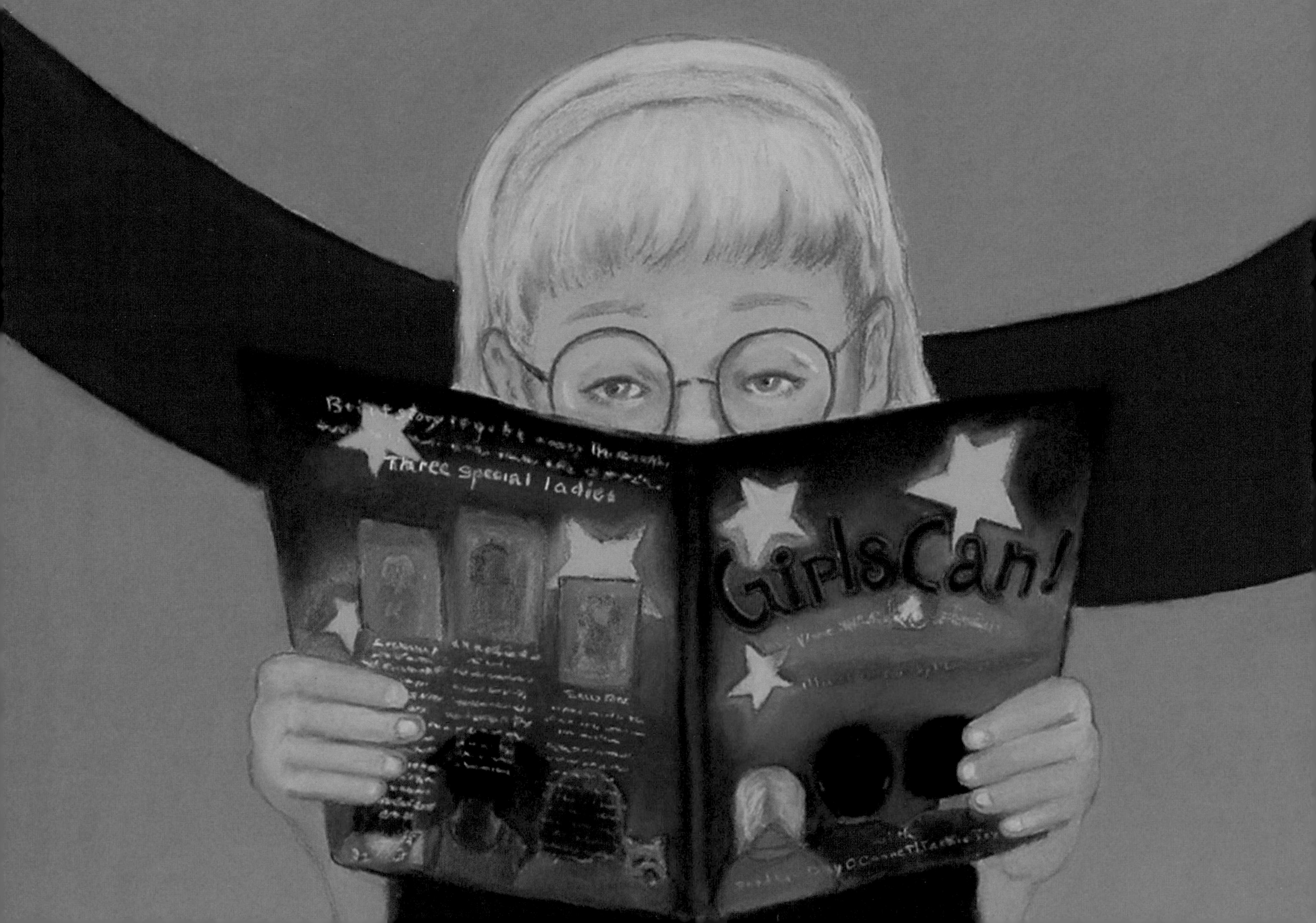

Of the **strong** little girl...
Who could run like no one else ever ran?

Have I told you the story...
Of the **smart** little girl...
Who grew up to help rule the whole land.

And there's that story I know...
Of the **brave** little girl...
Riding a rocket to the stars... was her plan.

These are the girls
I want you to know.
'Cause they showed all the world...

Girls CAN...

They can do Anything...

When they set their mind to it.
They just **Wish** it.
And then **Make** it so.

The thing about girls.
the ones that I know...
They're all winners.
Wherever they go.

Girls Rock...

They are strong.

SCIENCE FAIR

They are smart.

They should know it.
There's **Nothing** they just **Cannot** do.

It's taken too long

For the whole world to know it.

Let's change that.
And let's start with **you.**

I know a girl

She just **Loved** to **Run.**

She was the fastest fast runner around.

Little Jackie ran fast

faster Faster Fast Fast...

She blew past all the kids in the town.

She was focused — determined.
More than "all she could be"
Nobody could run like she ran.

This girl — running.
The best that she could.
Became the best of the best in the land.

Jackie says — **Find your passion!**

Whatever it is.

Find the thing
that makes you feel grand.

You do it for you.

Not for anyone else.

You're the one

who decides

your own plan!

Another girl I know...

She grew up on a ranch.
She rode horses before she could walk.

Sandra liked to read books
She had a pet pig
She chased rainbows — with her dad — in a truck.

She'd go to work with her dad
On the ranch everyday
And she'd help him however she could

She learned how to think...
And she learned how to talk...
And when she grew up... she got really good.

She took life step-by-step...

And she **Worked** all the way...

To the **Highest** court in the land.

She had no idea
She was going that way.
It's like life for her had its own plan.

Sandra said:

Find that **Thing!**

Find that one special **Thing!**

It's **Inside** you.

It's where you **Belong!**

Where it takes you

Won't matter so much.

the **Thing**... is what moves you along!

And I know a girl

She liked math most of all.
She could add & subtract all her numbers.

$$3.986 \times e^{-14} m \times 315 = 4e1.4$$

AT BAT 12 BALL 1 STRIKE 2 OUT 0
INNING 1 2 3 4 5 6 7 8 9 10
VISITOR 0
HOME 0 0

She also liked sports,
She knew all the names...
Of the guys who played for the Dodgers.

Sally played tennis.
She liked science.
And swimming.

She dreamed of places — away — so far...

And when she grew up

She took off for space.

On a rocket

Aimed right for a star.

You could **Not** tell her **No.**

She **Knew** she could do it.

Though no girl ever did it before.

That didn't bother Sally.
Not one little bit.
She believed she could do that — & more.

Because girls are Girls! They can Do anything.

They're every shape, color, size you can know.

The thing about girls...

They can **Be anything.**

When they get big... they can run the whole show.

Climb the mountain!
See the top!
Set your sights really high!

You are what – you decide – you will be.

And the way to be Great...
Is to set your Own course...
And see things the way they should be.

It won't be all easy.
It never has been.
You get "downs" with the "ups"
On the way.

That's no big deal really.
That's just how it works.
The "downs" are just steps on the way.

The thing to remember...

Remember this part...

You decide what you will be — today.

A mom. A doctor.
A writer of words.
The girl who's **Great** at ballet.

The teacher.
The baker.
The rancher.
The runner.
Or the astronaut who flies far away.

You might also decide...
"I'll just do what I do..."
And I'll figure it out on the way.

And you might change your mind.
Maybe once.
Maybe twice.
And you might know who you are — right away.

The **Best** thing to remember...
Wherever you go.
It's **YOU** driving.
You can **Go** your own way.

GIRLS CA

So Sit up!
Beep the horn!
Say — "Get outta my way!"
"You got a Girl here driving this car!"

Because nothing is better
Than a girl who knows

You are – who you are – who you are.